AFRICA DREAM

AFRICA DREAM

by Eloise Greenfield
illustrated by Carole Byard

HarperCollins*Publishers*

By the Author

Childtimes: A Three Generation Memoir *with Lessie Jones Little*
Honey, I Love and Other Love Poems
I Can Do It By Myself *with Lessie Jones Little*
Mary McLeod Bethune
Me and Neesie
Paul Robeson
Rosa Parks
She Come Bringing Me That Little Baby Girl
Sister
Under the Sunday Tree

Library of Congress Cataloging-in-Publication Data
Greenfield, Eloise. Africa dream.
SUMMARY: A black child's dreams are filled with
the images of the people and places of Africa.
[1. Africa—Fiction.] I. Byard, Carole M.   II. Title.
PZ7.G845Af   [E]   77-5080
ISBN 0-381-90061-4
ISBN 0-690-04776-2 (lib. bdg.)
ISBN 0-06-443277-7 (pbk.)

With love
To all children of African descent
May they find in their past the strength
to shape their future

I went all the way to Africa
In a dream one night
I crossed over the ocean
In a slow, smooth jump

And landed in Africa
Long-ago Africa

I went to the city
And shopped in the marketplace
For pearls and perfume

With magic eyes
I read strange words
In old books
And understood

I leaned small against
Tall stone buildings

And rode through the crowds
On a donkey's back

I dreamed I went to Africa
Long-ago Africa
I went to the village
And stood lonesome-still

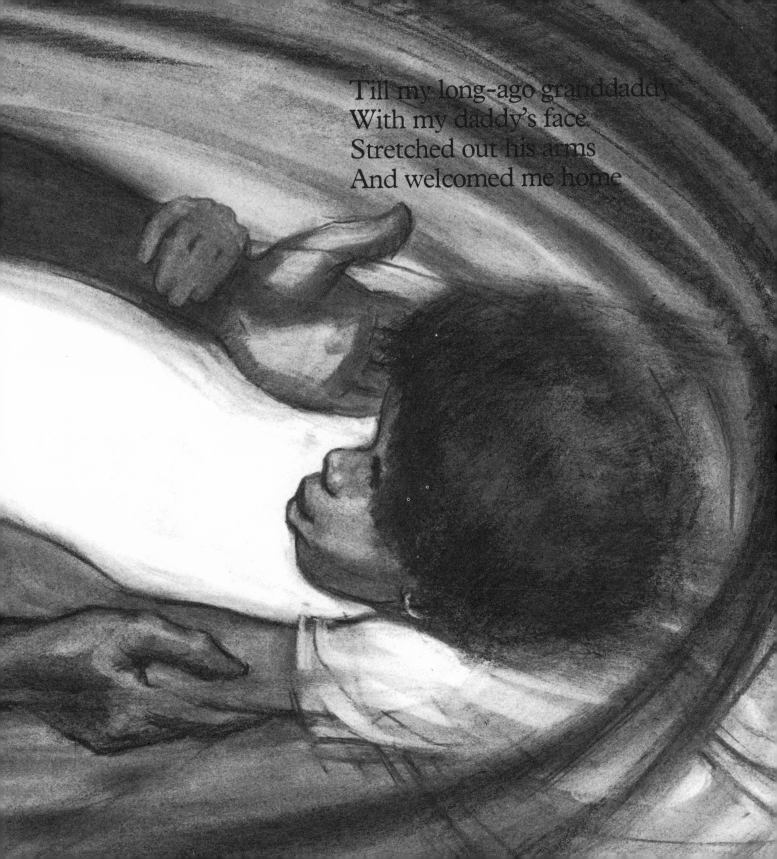

Till my long-ago granddaddy
With my daddy's face
Stretched out his arms
And welcomed me home

He knelt on one knee
And planted one seed
That grew into ten tall trees
With mangoes for me

I danced a hello dance
To the drums of my uncles

And sang a hello song
In a circle with new-old friends

I walked with my cousins
All over Africa
Lifting my long dress
To step across countries